BOTS

THE DRAGON BOTS

by Russ Bolts
Illustrated by Jay Cooper

LITTLE SIMON

New York London Toronto Sydney New Delhi

LITTLE SIMON
An imprint of Simon & Schuster Children's Publishing Division • 1230 Avenue of the Americas, New York, New York 10020 • First Little Simon hardcover edition July 2019 • Copyright © 2019 by Simon & Schuster, Inc. Also available in a Little Simon paperback edition. All rights reserved, including the right of reproduction in whole or in part in any form. LITTLE SIMON is a registered trademark of Simon & Schuster, Inc., and associated colophon is a trademark of Simon & Schuster, Inc. For information about special discounts for bulk purchases, please contact Simon & Schuster Special Sales at 1-866-506-1949 or business@simonandschuster.com. The Simon & Schuster Speakers Bureau can bring authors to your live event. For more information or to book an event contact the Simon & Schuster Speakers Bureau at 1-866-248-3049 or visit our website at www.simonspeakers.com. Designed by Nicholas Sciacca Manufactured in the United States of America 0120 FFG

2   4   6   8   10   9   7   5   3

Library of Congress Cataloging-in-Publication Data Names: Bolts, Russ, author. | Cooper, Jay, 1974– illustrator. Title: The dragon bots / by Russ Bolts ; illustrated by Jay Cooper. Description: First Little Simon paperback edition. | New York : Little Simon, 2019. | Series: Bots ; 4 | Summary: "Joe and Rob find themselves face to face with the magical Dragon Bots who have invaded their planet. Can they convince the Dragon Bots to become friends, or will all the Dragon Bots fry their circuits?"— Provided by publisher. Identifiers: LCCN 2019022099 | ISBN 9781534444195 (paperback) | ISBN 9781534444201 (hc) | ISBN 9781534444218 (ebook) Subjects: | CYAC: Robots—Fiction. | Dragons—Fiction. | Science fiction. | BISAC: JUVENILE FICTION / Dragons—FICTION / General. | JUVENILE FICTION / Robots. | JUVENILE Adventure / Readers / Chapter Books. Classification: LCC PZ7.1.B658 Dr 2019 | DDC [E]—dc23 LC record available at https://lccn.loc.gov/2019022099

CONTENTS

CHAPTER 1

No Such Thing

Warning! Warning!

The durgalmee-mees are about to attack!

I am running low on energy. Time to eat a power pellet!

1

Don't tell me that you have never dressed up like a Bot and played pretend before?

Here's a quick reminder of how we met the Bots:

Scientists

put space cameras

in rockets

that blasted into space

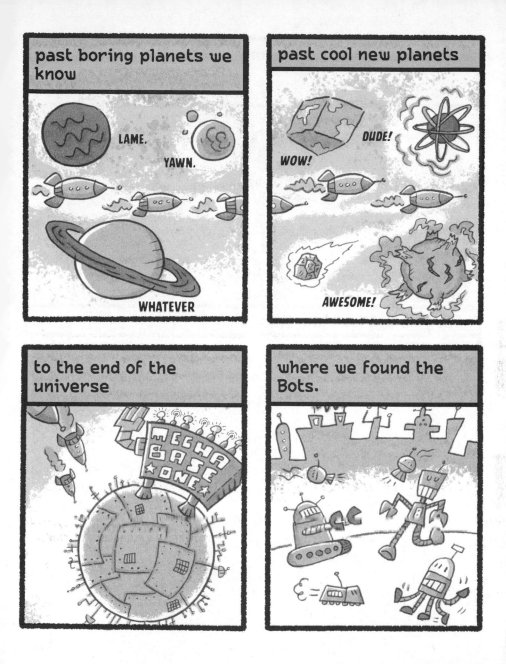

7

Let's check in on our favorite Bots, Joe and Rob.

They look like this.

They do not look like this.

Hmm, there is a lot of fog on Mecha Base One today.

Do you know about knights? We don't see them much anymore.

Maybe you are from a time when knights in shining armor rode on their horses and did whatever knights do?

Here's a picture of a knight.*

*If you look outside and see a person dressed like this, then this book has traveled back in time and you have found it. Congratulations! Read on to find out what you have to look forward to!

14

CHAPTER 2

...As Dragons?

And that is *not* a dragon.

It is a good thing that only we can see the Bots from our cameras. If anything on another planet watched this, they might think that the Bots are actual knights and wizards. They might think that dragons are real.

And we all know that there are no such things as dragons.

CHAPTER 3

Stray Signal

The space cameras work like this:
Record the Bots.

Make the video into a signal.

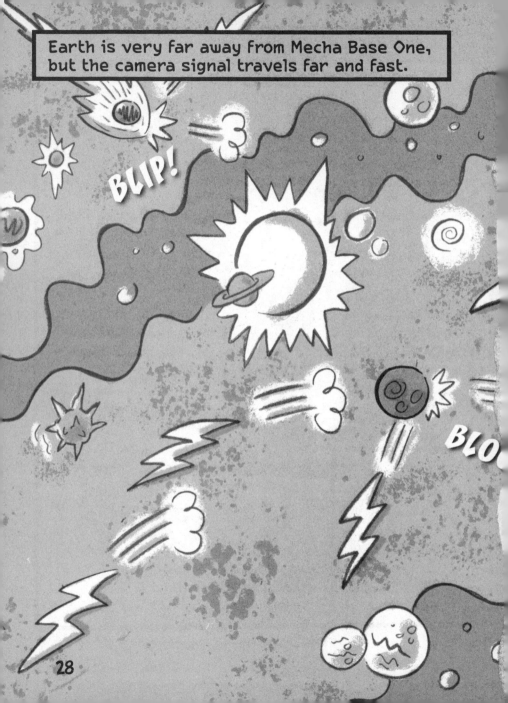

The signals are supposed to only travel to Earth. This way aliens or other life-forms in space won't know about the Bots . . . or about life on Earth.

Technically there *could* be stray signals. These are signals that travel to the other space cameras that were lost during the flight to Mecha Base One.

That would be bad.

But what are the chances that other life-forms found our space cameras?

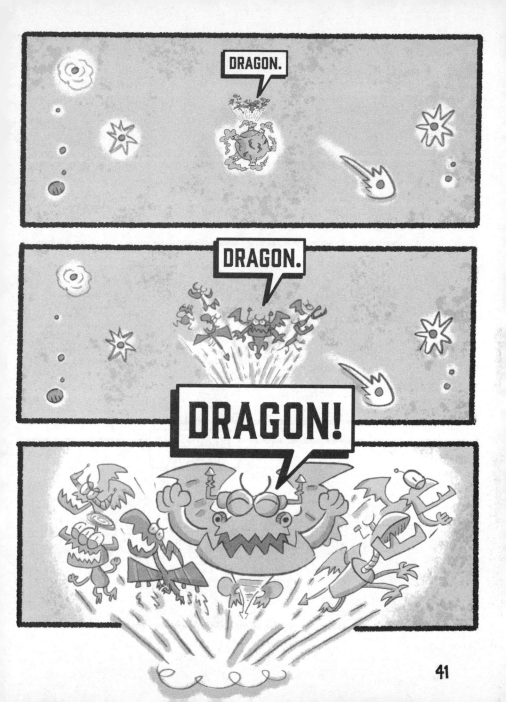

41

44

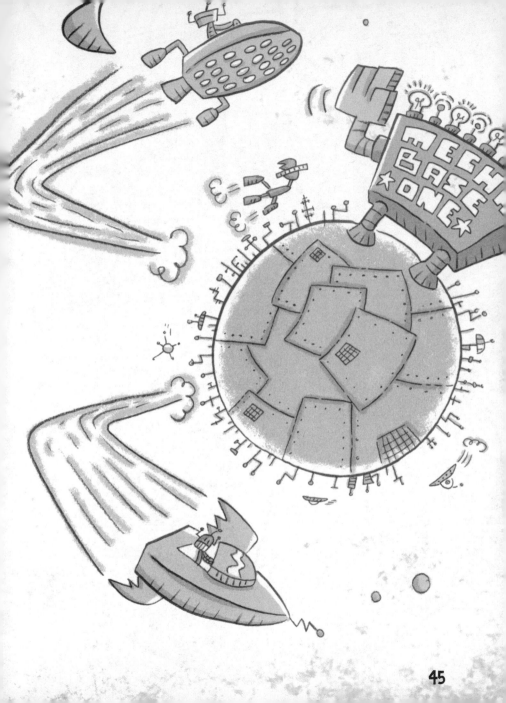

MECH BASE ONE

50

57

Oh dear. It seems like our space cameras landed in new worlds other than Mecha Base One . . . or should I call this planet Mecha Base *Done*?

CHAPTER 6
Scorcher!

Fellow humans, we have a name for very hot days on Earth. We call them scorchers.

We do not have a name for a fire-breathing dragon invasion. Maybe we should call *that* a scorcher?

We need to think fast, Joe.
What happens if we think slow?

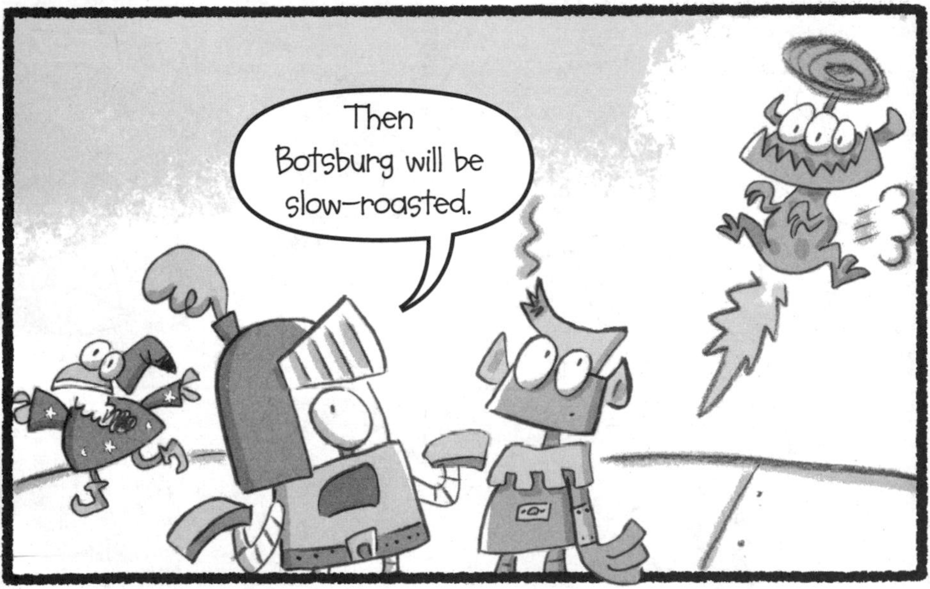
Then Botsburg will be slow-roasted.

65

73

Tinny and
the Dragon Bots
...
5 minutes ago.

81

FIRE

DANCE CLASS

YUM

95

Look at that. The Bots and the Dragon Bots are playing together and it looks like fun!

103

CHAPTER 10

Beast Friends

119

And as the Bots played on with the Dragon Bots, everyone had a scorching good time.

Well, almost everyone.

Yar. My Sea Plus Serpent is no match for flying Dragon Bots. Maybe the next adventure will be about Pi-robots and I'll have my time to shine.

123

TUNE IN NEXT TIME FOR...

#5

BOTS

A TALE OF TWO CLASSROOMS

by Russ Bolts   illustrated by Jay Cooper